Ruth
the Red Riding Hood
Fairy

To Harriet Matthews, with love

Special thanks to Rachel Elliot

Copyright © 2016 by Rainbow Magic Limited.

All rights reserved. Published by Scholastic Inc., *Publishers since 1920*. SCHOLASTIC and associated logos are trademarks and/or registered trademarks of Scholastic Inc. RAINBOW MAGIC is a trademark of Rainbow Magic Limited. Reg. U.S. Patent & Trademark Office and other countries. HIT and the HIT logo are trademarks of HIT Entertainment Limited.

The publisher does not have any control over and does not assume any responsibility for author or third-party websites or their content.

No part of this publication may be reproduced, stored in a retrieval system, or transmitted in any form or by any means, electronic, mechanical, photocopying, recording, or otherwise, without written permission of the publisher. For information regarding permission, write to Scholastic Inc., Attention: Permissions Department, 557 Broadway, New York, NY 10012.

This book is a work of fiction. Names, characters, places, and incidents are either the product of the author's imagination or are used fictitiously, and any resemblance to actual persons, living or dead, business establishments, events, or locales is entirely coincidental.

ISBN 978-1-338-05505-4

10 9 8 7 6 5 4 3 2 1   17 18 19 20 21

Printed in the U.S.A.   40
First edition, March 2017

Ruth
the Red Riding Hood
Fairy

by Daisy Meadows

SCHOLASTIC INC.

The Fairyland Palace

Fairyland Library

The Three Bears' Cottage

Island

Thumbelina's Cottage

Storybook World

Rapunzel's Tower

Red Riding Hood's Grandmother's House

Red Riding Hood Woods

Jack Frost's Ice Castle

Storytelling Festival Site

Wetherbury Village

Riverbank

Story Barge

The fairies want stories to stay just the same.
But I've planned a funny and mischievous game.
I'll change all their tales without further ado,
By adding some tricks and a goblin or two!

The four magic stories will soon be improved
When everything that's nice and sweet is removed.
Their dull happy endings are ruined and lost,
For no one's as smart as handsome Jack Frost!

Contents

Fairy Tale in the Firelight   1

Scrambled Story   11

Tracking the Goblins   23

A Twisted Hammock   35

Frightened Frost   45

Back in the Library   55

Fairy Tale in the Firelight

"There's something so magical about a campfire," said Kirsty Tate, warming her hands as the flames flickered.

"I love staring into the flames," said her best friend, Rachel Walker. "If you look at them for long enough, you can start to see pictures in there."

1

The girls leaned against each other, feeling happy, sleepy, and relaxed. They had spent a wonderful weekend at the Wetherbury Storytelling Festival, but now it was Sunday evening and the fun was nearly at  an end. Together with the other children from the festival, they were sitting on logs in a circle around a campfire. Alana Yarn, one of their favorite authors, had helped organize the weekend, and she was sitting on a log, too. The girls had had a wonderful time getting to know her.

"So," said Alana, looking around the circle at them all. "Have you enjoyed the Storytelling Festival? What was the best part?"

Everyone nodded and started to call out their favorite moments.

"The only bad thing about the whole weekend is that it has to end," said Rachel.

Alana smiled.

"We still have one more storytelling session before you have to go home," she said.

There was a large wicker basket in front of her, and she began to rummage through it.

Rachel turned and smiled at Kirsty.

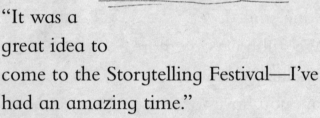

"Thank you for inviting me to stay this weekend," she said. "It was a great idea to come to the Storytelling Festival—I've had an amazing time."

"You're welcome," said Kirsty. "I'm really glad you came. I like everything ten times more when you're here. It's been an extra-special weekend."

Rachel nodded. "Especially because

we've had such a wonderful time with the Storybook Fairies," she whispered.

Rachel and Kirsty had shared lots of secret adventures with fairies, and meeting the Storybook Fairies had been enchanting. Elle the Thumbelina Fairy had whisked them away to the Fairyland Library, where they met Mariana the Goldilocks Fairy, Rosalie the Rapunzel Fairy, and Ruth the Red Riding Hood Fairy. The fairies were all very upset because Jack Frost and his goblins had stolen their magical objects, but Kirsty and Rachel had already helped get three of the objects back.

"I just hope that we can get Ruth's magical basket back soon," said Kirsty. "Until then, Jack Frost still has control of her story."

The fairies' objects gave the holder power over each story. Elle, Mariana, Rosalie, and Ruth always used their objects to make sure their fairy tales unfolded correctly. But Jack Frost and the goblins wanted the stories to be all about them. They had been using the magical objects to go *into* the stories and change them.

"We've gotten three of the objects back so far," said Rachel, thinking about their adventures during the festival. "There was Elle's thumb ring, Mariana's spoon, and Rosalie's hairbrush. If only we had already found Ruth's missing basket! Without it, I'm worried that Alana's final storytelling event will be ruined."

Just then, Alana Yarn cried, "Aha!" and pulled a red hooded cloak from her basket. She threw it around her shoulders with a flourish, and put up the hood. Her eyes twinkled in the firelight as she gazed around at the children. For a moment, no one spoke. They could hear the crackle of the burning twigs on the campfire. As the sun set behind the hills, the moon and stars began to shine.

"To close the
festival, we are
going to do
something very
special," Alana
said. "Everyone
is going to tell
a story together.
We will pass this
cloak around the
circle, and whoever
has it will tell part of the story. Does
anyone have any questions?"

"What else is in the basket?" called out
a girl with blond, curly hair.

Alana smiled. "There is a surprise
inside my basket, but that's for later.
Right now, we have a story to tell!"

The other kids laughed and whispered

with one another. They were eager to see what the surprise would be.

Kirsty and Rachel looked at each other, knowing that they were thinking the same thing: *Please don't let Jack Frost and his goblins ruin the story!*

Scrambled Story

"Let's begin," said Alana in an excited voice, taking out a red book and turning to the first page. "This beautiful cloak I'm wearing is a clue to which story we're going to tell. I will start you off, and let's see where the story takes us! Once upon a time ..."

She passed the cloak and the book to the girl next to her, who put on the cloak and read the next line from the book, ". . . there was a little girl who was called Red Riding Hood."

The boy next to her took the cloak and book and continued. "One day, Red Riding Hood's mother asked her to take some treats to her grandmother."

As the red cloak and the book were passed around the campfire circle, the story of Red Riding Hood unfolded and Rachel and Kirsty began to relax. Everything was happening exactly as it should. Maybe Ruth had already managed to find her magical basket! They listened as Red Riding Hood set off through the wood to her grandmother's house with a big basket of

goodies. Then the red cloak was passed to Rachel.

Feeling excited, Rachel slipped the heavy red cloak around her shoulders. It felt warm and she closed her eyes for a moment, thinking about all the things that she had learned about storytelling that weekend. Then she opened her eyes and started to read the next part of the story aloud.

"Red Riding Hood was halfway through the wood when she saw three figures on the path ahead. They were goblins!"

Rachel clapped her hand over her mouth, and Kirsty gasped in horror.

"Rachel, she meets a *wolf* in the wood, not goblins!" Kirsty whispered.

"I know!" Rachel groaned. "But the book says 'goblins'! And somehow I couldn't stop myself from reading it aloud!"

She quickly passed the cloak to Kirsty, who pulled it on and took the book, hoping that she could read the story without saying the word "goblin."

"Red Riding Hood knew that she shouldn't talk to strangers," Kirsty began, "but the goblins said—oh!"

Now it was Kirsty's turn to clap her hand over her mouth. She also hadn't been able to stop herself from saying "goblins" instead of "wolf"!

The girls looked around at the other children, but no one seemed to have noticed that anything strange had happened. Kirsty didn't dare to read more. She took off the cloak and passed it and the book to the children on the next log.

As a little boy put the cloak around his shoulders, Rachel nudged Kirsty.

"Look at Alana's basket!" she whispered.

The basket was glowing as if there was a fire inside it. The girls watched and saw a tiny fairy flutter out of it and shoot into the air.

"It's Ruth the Red Riding Hood Fairy!" Kirsty exclaimed.

Ruth was wearing a white dress with red stars around the hem, and a silky red cloak was swirling around

her shoulders. She had beautiful glasses with delicate black frames, magnifying her sparkling eyes.

Her brown hair gleamed in the firelight as she zoomed down to the girls and hid behind the log where they were sitting.

"Hello, Ruth," Rachel whispered out of the corner of her mouth. "It's good that you're here—something very strange is happening to the *Red Riding Hood* story."

"I know," Ruth whispered back. "I need

your help—and quickly! Will you come into the story with me now?"

The girls looked around at the other children. Everyone was watching a boy who was reading the next part of the story aloud.

"The goblins snatched Red Riding Hood's basket and blew a big raspberry at her," the boy was saying.

"Oh dear," said Kirsty in a low voice. "We really need to find those goblins. Luckily, no one's looking our way. Come on—let's go!"

Moving slowly so they wouldn't attract attention, Rachel and Kirsty slipped off the log and ducked out of sight. Ruth gave them a relieved smile.

"I already feel better just knowing you're going to help me," she said. "Elle,

Mariana, and Rosalie all said that they couldn't have gotten their magical objects back without you."

"We're just happy to be able to help," said Rachel. "We don't want the last event of the Storytelling Festival to be spoiled. We want to save stories for everyone!"

Ruth took out a little
red book. The
words *Red
Riding
Hood* were
written
in silver
letters on
the front,
and they
sparkled in
the light from the
campfire. Ruth held up her wand and
spoke.

"*The storybook world is in danger
today.*

"*We must find the goblins and send
them away.*

"Take me and my friends to the path through the wood,

"And help us to rescue dear Red Riding Hood."

The campfire, the other children, and the twinkling stars disappeared as if someone had blown them away. Instead, Rachel and Kirsty found themselves standing on a narrow, winding path, surrounded by crowded fir trees on both sides. They were inside the storybook world once more.

Tracking the Goblins

Ruth fluttered between Rachel and
Kirsty as they gazed around. In the
storybook world, the girls were still
human-size. Bright sunlight filtered
through the leaves, and bluebells and
poppies grew in colorful patches among
the trees.

"How beautiful," said Kirsty.

"Listen!" Rachel exclaimed, putting a hand on her friend's arm. "I can hear someone coming."

The girls darted out of sight behind a tree, and Ruth perched on Kirsty's shoulder. Seconds later, a little girl came skipping around a bend in the path.

She was swinging a wicker basket as she skipped, and her red cloak swirled around her shoulders. She was singing a song to herself.

"Red Riding Hood!" Rachel whispered in a thrilled voice.

"She's such a happy girl," said Ruth with a smile.

Suddenly there was a cacophony of screeches, squeals, and whoops, and three goblins leaped out of the wood and danced around Red Riding Hood. She gasped and turned from left to right, trying to get away from them. But one of the goblins grabbed at her cloak.

"No, that's mine!" she cried.

But the goblin just laughed at her and pulled the cloak from her shoulders. Her basket was knocked to the ground, and muffins, cookies, and fruit scattered all around. The goblins ran off into the wood, shrieking in delight.

"Hey, stop!" cried Red Riding Hood. "Bring back my cloak! Thieves!"

She started to chase them, but she tripped over a tree root and fell onto the leafy ground.

Rachel and Kirsty darted out from behind the tree and helped Red Riding Hood to her feet.

Her knees were dirty and her dress was torn.

"Are you all right?" Kirsty asked.

"Yes, I'm fine," said Red Riding Hood. "They just surprised me. My mother warned me that there were wolves in the wood. But she didn't say anything about strange green creatures like that."

"They're so mean," said Rachel. "Don't worry—we'll help you pick up your things."

Kirsty and Red Riding Hood gathered armfuls of the fruit and baked goods, and Ruth picked up the cloth that had covered all the food. Rachel picked up the basket, which had rolled to one side of the path, and looked at it carefully. Her heart gave a sudden hopeful thump of excitement.

"Ruth, could this be your magical basket?" she asked.

Ruth shook her head.

"Mine glitters with magic," she said. "Besides, we know that Jack Frost and his goblins have it."

The girls packed the food back into the basket, and then Ruth tucked the cloth over everything.

"Thank you," said Red Riding Hood. "You're very kind. But I'm so sad to have lost my cloak. My grandmother made it for me, and I always wear it."

"The goblins have stolen something belonging to Ruth, too," said Kirsty. "We have to get it back! If we can catch them, we will get your cloak back, too."

"Thank you!" said Red Riding Hood. "But I must hurry—my grandmother will be waiting for me."

Red Riding Hood waved and went on her way. As she disappeared along the winding path, Rachel heard a distant, high-pitched giggle.

"Goblins!" she exclaimed. "I'd know that sound anywhere. If we're quick, we can still catch up with them."

"They might lead us to your magical basket, Ruth," Kirsty added.

"Good thinking," said Ruth. "And wings are quicker than feet!"

She waved her wand, and a shower of silvery sparkles erupted from the tip. Covered in fairy dust, Rachel and Kirsty twirled around as they shrank to fairy size. Their delicate wings unfurled

and fluttered, shaking the last sparkles
of fairy dust onto the path through the
wood.

They rose into the air and listened.
Somewhere ahead of them, among the
trees, the goblins were still giggling.

"Come on, we don't want to lose them!"
cried Ruth.

They flew over the treetops, guided by

the giggles. Soon they spotted the three goblins below. One of them was wearing the red cloak and pretending to be Red Riding Hood, skipping along and singing in a silly, squeaky voice. The others were shrieking with laughter and jumping around, making faces.

"Those troublemakers!" Kirsty exclaimed. "I wonder where they're going."

"Let's get closer," said Rachel.

They weaved among the trees, staying behind the goblins and listening as they

giggled and teased one another. Then
they reached a clearing, where a tall oak
tree was growing among the firs. A blue
hammock swung from the branches, and
the goblins stopped and stared at it. The
fairies stopped, too, their wings fluttering
fast as they hovered.

"Why have they gone so quiet?" Ruth
asked in a whisper.

The hammock moved, and the goblins
took a step back. Then a pair of familiar,
angry eyes appeared over the hammock's
edge.

"It's about time!" snarled Jack Frost,
sitting up.

"Oh my goodness!" Kirsty cried. "Look
what he has on his lap."

It was Ruth's glittering magical basket!

A Twisted Hammock

"We have to get it back," Rachel said in a determined voice. "Come on!"

The three fairies swooped down toward the basket, hoping that they could reach it before they were seen. But the goblin in the cloak glanced up and spotted them.

"Ooh!" he squeaked, jumping up and down and pointing. "Ooh! Ooooh!"

Jack Frost looked up and rolled his eyes.

"Stop saying 'Ooh!', you fool!" he snapped. "They're fairies, not fireworks!"

He clutched the basket to his chest and pointed a long, bony finger at the fairies.

"You get out of here!" he shouted. "Swat them away, goblins! Get them!"

Kirsty dived under the hammock and the goblin in the cloak lunged after her.

Kirsty darted out of his way, and he hurled himself against the hammock by mistake.

"EEEK!" yelled Jack Frost as the hammock spun over and over, wrapping him up inside it.

"WAHHHH!" wailed the goblin as Red Riding Hood's cloak was tangled into the hammock.

Seconds later, when the hammock stopped spinning, Jack Frost and the goblin were knotted together, their legs and arms sticking out at strange angles.

"We should grab the basket while he can't use his hands to stop us!" said Ruth.

"The basket is buried somewhere inside that hammock," said Kirsty. "We'll have to wait."

She led Rachel and Ruth up to a tree branch above.

"How are we ever going to get my magical basket back?" Ruth asked with a groan.

Rachel and Kirsty couldn't answer, because Jack Frost was shrieking too loudly, his voice getting higher and higher with each word.

"How dare you tie me up? Who did this? When I get out of here, you are going to be in so much trouble!"

The goblin in the red cloak was also yelling, but his voice was too muffled to be understood. The other two goblins hid behind the oak's trunk, their knees knocking together.

"Those poor goblins," said Rachel. "It's not their fault that he got all tangled up.

I know they're troublemakers, but they don't deserve to be shouted at like that. Jack Frost needs a good scare himself."

"That gives me an idea," said Kirsty. "I know who would scare Jack Frost— the wolf!"

"You're right," said Ruth, looking thoughtful. "And the best person to help lure the wolf to where we want him is Red Riding Hood."

"Yes!" said Rachel, clapping her hands together. "If we can get the wolf to come to the oak tree and scare Jack Frost, we might be able to grab the magical basket."

"Come on, there's no time to lose!" Kirsty exclaimed. "We have to catch up with Red Riding Hood!"

The three fairies zoomed into the sky

as fast as
arrows, and
flew over the
treetops until
they saw the
winding path
below them once
again. Red Riding Hood was
hurrying along, but she wasn't skipping
now. Rachel, Kirsty, and Ruth swooped
down and hovered in front of her.

"Oh, hello again!" said Red Riding
Hood, frowning a little. "Weren't you
human beings a few minutes ago?"

"It's magic," Ruth explained.

"Oh, I see," said Red Riding Hood.
"That explains it."

In the storybook world, no one was
surprised by magic.

"We've come to ask for your help," said Kirsty. "We want to get the wolf to go to the big oak tree in the middle of the wood. We think he might be able to help us get Ruth's basket and your cloak back from the goblins."

"Will you help us?" asked Ruth. "Please?"

"Of course," said Red Riding Hood at once. "I'll do anything I can to get my cloak back and stop those goblins!"

"Fantastic," Ruth cried. She did a twirl in midair. "We haven't a minute to lose!"

Frightened Frost

Red Riding Hood and the fairies quickly worked out a plan. Then Rachel, Kirsty, and Ruth fluttered up to hide in the treetops.

"Tra la la," sang Red Riding Hood in a loud voice. "I can't wait to see my grandmother! I'm sure she'll love this big basket of goodies I'm taking to her."

The leaves on the other side of the path rustled, and then a large gray wolf stepped out. He bared his teeth and licked them with a long, pink tongue.

"He looks very scary!" said Rachel with a shudder. "What big teeth he has!"

"Where does your grandmother live, little girl?" asked the wolf in a gruff voice.

Red Riding Hood pointed the way through the wood toward the big oak tree.

"Granny lives that way," she said.

The wolf didn't wait to listen to

anything else. With one bound he was
charging into the wood, speeding toward
the clearing where the fairies had left
Jack Frost.

"Quickly—don't lose sight of him!"
Rachel cried.

The three fairies flew above him,
and Red Riding Hood ran along behind
him as quickly as she could. The wolf was
very fast.

"He'll be at the oak tree soon," said Ruth. "Let's fly ahead!"

They zoomed toward the clearing and saw that Jack Frost and the goblin with the cloak had managed to get untangled. Jack Frost was once again relaxing in his hammock.

"Look, he still has the magical basket!" said Kirsty.

Jack Frost was twirling the glittering basket on the tip of his forefinger, chuckling. Beneath the swinging hammock, the three goblins were busy cheating at a card game.

"I showed them!" Jack Frost crowed. "I showed those silly fairies! They just flew away because they were so scared of me. Ha!"

HOWWWWL! The wolf leaped into the

clearing. Jack Frost let out a high-pitched squeal and sprang out of his hammock. The magical basket fell down and rolled across the ground.

"The basket!" screeched the goblin with the cloak.

"Never mind that," shouted Jack Frost. "RUN!"

The goblins darted after him, and in their panic the cloak dropped onto the ground. Ruth swooped down to seize her basket, and it shrank to fairy size as soon as she touched it.

"Let's get the cloak!" said Rachel.

She and Kirsty fluttered down and picked up the cloak between them. The wolf howled again, just as Red Riding Hood arrived in the clearing, out of breath.

"Here's your cloak," said Kirsty, flying over to Red Riding Hood.

She and Rachel carefully draped the cloak around the girl's shoulders. Then Red Riding Hood turned to the wolf.

"I'm sorry," she said. "I got confused about the direction to my grandmother's house. It's actually just down that path."

She pointed down a narrow path through the wood, which the fairies hadn't noticed before. Through the leaves, they could just see the chimney of a little cottage.

The wolf dashed off along the path, and Red Riding Hood followed, skipping slowly and swinging her basket.

"The story is back to normal," said Ruth. "Now everything will start to happen just as it should."

"I hope Red Riding Hood will be all right," said Kirsty. "That wolf is pretty scary."

"Don't worry," said Rachel, smiling at her. "Remember the story? Red Riding

Hood and her grandmother manage to trick the wolf and escape. And we know that will happen, because the magical basket is back with its rightful owner."

"Come on," Ruth said, fluttering over to join Rachel and Kirsty. "We have somewhere wonderful to go!"

Back in the Library

Ruth waved her wand, and the storybook wood around them vanished. They were once again standing in the beautiful Fairyland Library. Rachel and Kirsty gazed around in wonder and delight at the high shelves filled with books and the arched glass ceiling. Standing in front of them were Elle the Thumbelina

Fairy, Mariana the Goldilocks Fairy, and Rosalie the Rapunzel Fairy. Ruth rushed over to them, and they all hugged her.

She placed her magical basket carefully into the wooden box where it belonged, and closed the golden clasp. Then all four of the Storybook Fairies turned to Rachel and Kirsty.

"You two have been wonderful," said Elle.

"All our magical objects are safe again, and we have you to thank," added Mariana.

"We will never forget what you have done for us," said Rosalie.

Ruth stepped forward and gave each girl a kiss on the cheek. She was about to speak, but before she could say a word there was a thunderclap and a bright, icy blue flash. The fairies were dazzled and had to shade their eyes. When they looked, they saw Jack Frost standing in the middle of the library. His frown was worse than ever.

"You've messed up *everything*!" he yelled. "All I wanted was to be the star of my very own story. I made those stories a million times better and you've ruined them!"

"You can still be the star of a story," said Rachel.

"Not without the Storybook Fairies' magical objects I can't," he snarled. "Give them to me!"

"You *can* be the star," Rachel insisted. "You just have to make up the story yourself. Don't ruin stories that already exist. Make up something new!"

"Everyone loves the fairy tales that the Storybook Fairies protect," Kirsty added. "We can't allow you to change them. But I bet you could make up a great story about your own adventures."

She saw a notepad and a pencil lying on one of the library tables. Smiling, she picked them up and handed them to Jack Frost. He hesitated, and then took them as a grin spread across his face.

"My own adventures," he muttered. "It'll be an epic tale. I'll be a brave hero, surrounded by green fools. Yes, I can see it now! *The Adventures of Jack Frost*!"

He sat down and began to write his own storybook world. With a smile, Ruth turned back to Rachel and Kirsty.

"To thank you for everything you've done for us, we have something very special to give each of you," she said.

She handed each girl a small card. On one side, the cards glimmered with the changing colors of the rainbow. On the other, in golden letters, were the words:

Member of the Fairyland Library

"You will always be welcome here," Ruth said to them. "You may borrow one book at a time, and although you will be able to read it, no one else in the human world will be able to see it."

"Thank you!" said Rachel and Kirsty together, feeling awed.

Ruth raised her wand once more.

"Now it is time for us to say good-bye," she said. "But I hope we will see you again soon—on your next library visit!"

She swished her wand, and the bright library vanished. It was replaced by twinkling stars and flickering flames. The

girls were back at the Storybook Festival.

Rachel and Kirsty listened in delight as the other children finished telling the story of *Red Riding Hood*. This time, Red Riding Hood met a wolf in the wood, and there was no mention of goblins anywhere. The girls exchanged smiles of relief.

"Who wants to toast marshmallows?" called Alana. "I brought some in my basket."

Soon, the children and Alana were enjoying the sweet, sticky warmth of toasted marshmallows.

"Now," Alana said, licking her lips. "Would anyone like to try out what they have learned at the festival? I would love to hear any stories that you have imagined."

Rachel's hand shot into the air.

"Kirsty and I have a story to tell," she said.

"What's it about?" a little boy asked.

Rachel gave a mysterious smile.

"Magic," she said.

Together, the best friends told a tale
of brave fairies and naughty goblins.
The other children gasped and laughed
as they listened to the story. When
Kirsty said the words "and they all lived
happily ever after," everyone cheered
and clapped.

"That was a fabulous story," said
Alana. "I'm really
impressed by
your amazing
imaginations!"

Rachel
and Kirsty
exchanged a
secret smile. They

knew that they hadn't imagined the story!

"I wonder when we'll have more magical adventures," said Rachel.

"Very soon," Kirsty said, feeling certain. "And I can't wait for the next one to begin!"

RAINBOW
magic

SPECIAL EDITION

Rachel and Kirsty have found the
Storybook Fairies' missing magic objects.
Now it's time for them to help

Alicia
the Snow Queen Fairy!

Join their next adventure in
this special sneak peek ...

Dull December

"What an icy, gray December this is," said Rachel Walker, blowing on her fingers and shivering. "I'm starting to wonder if it will ever be Christmas!"

It was Saturday morning, and Rachel was in her backyard with her best friend,

Kirsty Tate. They had come out to play a game of ball, but sleet was coming down. Kirsty shivered, too, and buried her hands deep into her pockets.

"I'm really glad I'm staying with you for the weekend, but I wish the weather wasn't so horrible," Kirsty said.

"We had such awesome plans," said Rachel. "But nature walks and boating on the lake won't be much fun when it's so miserable and freezing. It looks as if we'll be spending most of the weekend inside."

"Never mind," said Kirsty, smiling at her friend. "We always have fun when we're together, no matter what we're doing."

"You're right," said Rachel, trying to forget about the dark clouds above.

"Let's go inside," Kirsty said. "I think it's starting to snow."

"Oh, really?" said Rachel, feeling more cheerful. "Maybe we can go sledding."

"I don't think so," said Kirsty. "I only see one snowflake."

She pointed up to the single, perfect snowflake. It was spiraling down from the gray sky. The girls watched it land on the edge of a stone birdbath.

"That's funny," said Rachel after a moment. "It's not melting."

Kirsty took a step closer to the birdbath. "I think it's getting bigger," she said.

The snowflake began to grow bigger and bigger. Then it popped like a snowy balloon, and the girls saw a tiny fairy standing in its place. She was as exquisite as the snowflake had been. Her blond hair flowed around her shoulders, and she was wearing a long blue gown, decorated with sparkling silver sequins. A furry cape was wrapped around her shoulders, and a snowflake tiara twinkled on her head.

"Hello, Rachel and Kirsty," said the fairy. "I'm Alicia the Snow Queen Fairy."

"Hello, Alicia!" said Rachel. "It's great to meet you!"

"What are you doing here in Tippington?" Kirsty asked.

"I've come to ask for your help," said Alicia in a silvery voice.

RAINBOW magic™

Which Magical Fairies Have You Met?

- ☐ The Rainbow Fairies
- ☐ The Weather Fairies
- ☐ The Jewel Fairies
- ☐ The Pet Fairies
- ☐ The Sports Fairies
- ☐ The Ocean Fairies
- ☐ The Princess Fairies
- ☐ The Superstar Fairies
- ☐ The Fashion Fairies
- ☐ The Sugar & Spice Fairies
- ☐ The Earth Fairies
- ☐ The Magical Crafts Fairies
- ☐ The Baby Animal Rescue Fairies
- ☐ The Fairy Tale Fairies
- ☐ The School Day Fairies

RAINBOW magic™

SPECIAL EDITION

Which Magical Fairies Have You Met?

- ❏ Joy the Summer Vacation Fairy
- ❏ Holly the Christmas Fairy
- ❏ Kylie the Carnival Fairy
- ❏ Stella the Star Fairy
- ❏ Shannon the Ocean Fairy
- ❏ Trixie the Halloween Fairy
- ❏ Gabriella the Snow Kingdom Fairy
- ❏ Juliet the Valentine Fairy
- ❏ Mia the Bridesmaid Fairy
- ❏ Flora the Dress-Up Fairy
- ❏ Paige the Christmas Play Fairy
- ❏ Emma the Easter Fairy
- ❏ Cara the Camp Fairy
- ❏ Destiny the Rock Star Fairy
- ❏ Belle the Birthday Fairy
- ❏ Olympia the Games Fairy

- ❏ Selena the Sleepover Fairy
- ❏ Cheryl the Christmas Tree Fairy
- ❏ Florence the Friendship Fairy
- ❏ Lindsay the Luck Fairy
- ❏ Brianna the Tooth Fairy
- ❏ Autumn the Falling Leaves Fairy
- ❏ Keira the Movie Star Fairy
- ❏ Addison the April Fool's Day Fairy
- ❏ Bailey the Babysitter Fairy
- ❏ Natalie the Christmas Stocking Fairy
- ❏ Lila and Myla the Twins Fairies
- ❏ Chelsea the Congratulations Fairy
- ❏ Carly the School Fairy
- ❏ Angelica the Angel Fairy
- ❏ Blossom the Flower Girl Fairy
- ❏ Skyler the Fireworks Fairy
- ❏ Giselle the Christmas Ballet Fairy

SCHOLASTIC

Find all of your favorite fairy friends at
scholastic.com/rainbowmagic

3 stories in each one!

HIT entertainment

RMSPECIAL